Safari
Animals

For Karen Scawen

Many thanks to the staff and children at
Discovery Montessori Day Nursery, Burnham, Berkshire
and Teeny Tots Nursery, Slough, Berkshire
for their help and advice.

This edition first published 2009
by Zero to Ten, part of Evans Publishing Group
2A Portman Mansions, Chiltern St, London W1U 6NR
and 814 North Franklin Street, Chicago Illinois 60610, USA

Reprinted 2010 (twice)

A CIP catalogue record for this book is available from the British Library.

Library of Congress CIP data applied for.

ISBN 9781840895629

Printed by Grafo, S. A. in Basauri, Spain, November 2010, job number (CAG1640)

Safari
Animals

Illustrated by

Paul Hess

Zebra

Observing them is difficult,
one quickly loses track
of whether they are black on white
or rather, white on black.

Rhino

"Griffy, gruffy,"
Goes the rhinoceros.
His horns are pointy
And his feet are thunderous.

Hyena

Hyenas laugh until they choke

But never want to share the joke...

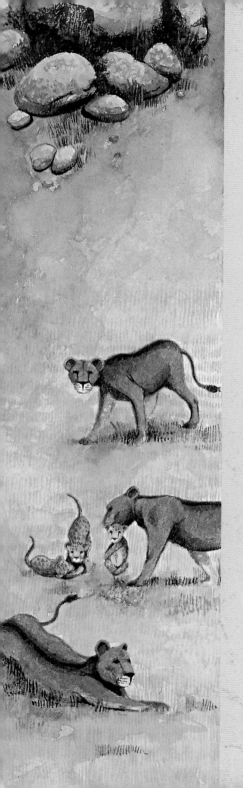

Lion

The Lion has a golden mane
and under it a clever brain.
He lies around and idly roars
and lets the lioness do the chores.

Vulture

His eye is dull, his head is bald,

His neck is growing thinner.

Oh! what a lesson for us all

To only eat at dinner!

Leopard

The leopard is the sort of cat
You shouldn't keep inside a flat...
He's happiest when running free
Or sleeping in a sun-baked tree.

Wildebeest

The magnificent wildebeest,

Wander in herds to follow the rains,

Grazing on the sweet, sweet grass,

That grows on the Serengeti plains.

Elephant

Way down South where bananas grow,

A grasshopper stepped on an elephant's toe.

The elephant said, with tears in his eyes,

"Pick on somebody your own size."

Farmyard Animals
ISBN 9781840895599

Safari Animals
ISBN 9781840895629

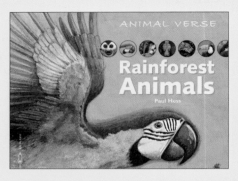

Rainforest Animals
ISBN 9781840895605

Polar Animals
ISBN 9781840895612

If you have any problems obtaining any title, or would like to receive information about our books, please contact the publishers:
Zero To Ten, Evans Publishing Group, 2A Portman Mansions, Chiltern St, London W1U 6NR Tel 020 7487 0920 Fax 020 7487 0921 or
814 North Franklin Street, Chicago, Illinois 60610 Toll Free Order Tel: (800) 888-IPG1 (4741) All other inquiries: (312) 337 0747 Fax: (312) 337 5985